Two at the Net

Library of Congress Cataloging in Publication Data
Sheffer, H. R.
Two at the net.
(Teammates)
SUMMARY: An excellent tennis player, Dee must decide whether to devote her life to the game or make time for some of the things other high school girls enjoy.
(1. Tennis--Fiction) I. Schroeder, Howard. II. Vista III Design. III. Title. IV. Series.
PZ7.A1595Tw (Fic) 80-28429
ISBN 0-89686-108-2 (lib. bdg.)
ISBN 0-89686-118-X (pbk.)

International Standard Book Numbers:
0-89686-108-2 Library Bound
0-89686-118-X Paperback

Library of Congress Catalog Card Number:
80-28429

Box 3427
Hwy. 66 South
Mankato, MN 56001

Two at the Net

BY H.R. SHEFFER

ILLUSTRATED BY VISTA III DESIGN

EDITED BY DR. HOWARD SCHROEDER
Professor in Reading and Language Arts
Dept. of Elementary Education
Mankato State University

CRESTWOOD HOUSE
Mankato, Minnesota

Two at the Net

Dee Caruso tossed a ball in the air and served it across the net to Angie Morabito. Angie drove it back, hitting the ball easily so that it fell well within the foul lines. Quickly, Dee raced to the front court, slamming her return shot into the opposite court. It caught Angie off-guard.

"Forty-thirty," Dee called, brushing at the damp strands of hair that clung to her forehead. She felt for the sweatband around her head and pushed it closer to her eyebrows.

The afternoon air was unusually warm for May. Heat reflected back from the clay flooring of the school's tennis courts.

Dee took the next point, winning the game and set. It was the second set they had played since school let out an hour before.

"One more and we'll call it quits," she called to Angie.

"Forget it!" Angie was tired. "I'm good, but I can't keep up with you, Caruso. You're the best!"

Dee enjoyed hearing Angie's words. She was the best, and she knew it — at least, she was the

best around here. No one else in the Jamestown area could begin to keep up with her on a tennis court. Ever since she was ten years old and her father had first placed a tennis racket in her hand, Dee had known that she wanted someday to be a professional. She played well and she played to win.

For several years her father had been her only teacher and coach. But Jamestown High was lucky to have a former tennis pro as one of its physical education teachers. Coach Riley had organized a tennis team when he first started at Jamestown eight years before. Now, with tennis booming around the country, a league had been set up. Jamestown had developed one of the best teams in that league.

Last year Dee had won the junior championship for the area. Now finals were approaching again, and this time Dee knew she would take the biggest trophy of all; the senior girl's championship.

The elimination trials had been going on for weeks. Dee had won all of her matches, as had Angie. Now they were looking forward to the following week when the final games were scheduled.

"Are you two quitting already?" Coach Riley asked as he came up the path to the courts. Link Olson and Alan Qwan were with him. "You're just

the two I was looking for," Coach Riley said as he entered the court.

Dee looked past him and smiled at Link. Link Olson was the star of Jamestown's men's team. With his thick blond hair and bright blue eyes, he looked the part of the all-American tennis player. But although Link enjoyed tennis and played well, it was not the most important thing in his life.

Dee had little time for dating since she was in training most of the time. But when she did accept a rare invitation, it was usually from Link Olson. Deep down she wished that she had a lot more time to spend with Link. She knew that if things went that way, he could become very important to her.

"I'm pairing you two up," Coach Riley said, pulling Link to stand next to Dee.

For a moment she was startled, wondering if he could read her mind. But then she realized what he was talking about. The following weekend, after the singles finals, there would be an exhibition doubles game. There wasn't a trophy for the doubles. However, it had become one of the favorite events in the tourney. Each school sent their best couples and opponents were chosen by draw. Because the results were not counted, little time was given to matching up the players beforehand.

"Link, you and Dee will be one of our teams, and Alan and Angie will be the other. I don't want you to spend too much time on this, but for the next week try and get in a couple of doubles games together. You will need the practice. There are a lot of differences in the two games, as you all know. Doubles is a faster, harder game." Coach Riley nodded his head at them and walked away.

Link slipped his arm around Dee's shoulders. "Well, I lucked out again," he said, giving her a big grin.

Alan looked at Angie. "I didn't do too badly, either," he said, and they all laughed.

"Come on," Dee urged. "It's only 4:30 p.m. Let's get in some practice."

"No, Dee," Angie said. "I'm exhausted! Let's do it tomorrow."

"We'll do it tomorrow, too," Dee declared. "And if you're exhausted it means you're out of shape. Come on!"

"Humor her," Link said. "I know this girl. She never gives up. She'll drive us crazy until we agree."

"All right," Angie gave in. "But only for a little while. I really have to be home by 5:30 p.m."

Alan smiled at her. "Big date tonight?"

"Right," said Angie. "And I'm not going to be late for it because of a tennis game."

They took their positions on the court and as they did, Dee thought, that's the difference between Angie and me. A date is more important to her. A game is more important to me.

They took their places on opposite courts. Dee and Angie were in the front courts, Link and Alan were in the back.

"Let's just volley," called Alan. "We don't have enough time to play a regulation game. Besides, we should get used to playing tennis with each other."

"Good idea," Dee agreed. "Then tomorrow we can get into a serious game."

The others looked at her, Angie and Alan with grins, and Link was smiling, too. But, there was a question in his eyes.

Alan served the first ball. For a few minutes they volleyed back and forth across the net. Dee easily returned the short lobs while Link took care of the back court. Several of his returns were net balls. Before she realized it, Dee was concentrating on winning over the other team. She started chasing every ball that was near her. Often Dee found herself backing up and taking them away from Link.

The action of the game picked up as Angie and Alan tried to meet her rhythm.

There was a sudden shout from Link. "Hey,

wait a minute!" he cried. "What's going on here? This was supposed to be an easy practice game."

Dee spun around to face him, her concentration broken. "What are you talking about?" She was annoyed that he had stopped the game.

He glanced down at his wristwatch. "It's getting late. I have to get home. We can pick this up again tomorrow or later in the week." He walked slowly off the court, picking up a towel from the bench.

"Thank goodness," Angie groaned. "I really have to get going." She grabbed her sweater that had been tossed across the back of a bench.

"Come on. I'll give you a ride," Alan said. "I'm going your way." He turned to look at Link and Dee. "Anybody else need a way home?"

Dee shook her head. "No, thanks. I'd rather walk."

"I'll keep her company," Link said. "Thanks anyhow."

The other two raced off toward the school parking lot.

Link turned to Dee. "Are you hungry?" he asked.

"Of course I'm hungry," Dee said, putting her arms into her sweater. "It's almost dinner time."

"I meant, would you like to stop and have something to eat on our way home?"

Dee looked at him in surprise. "Now? My mother would kill me if I did that."

"Well, how about stopping for a soft drink or something?"

Dee was torn. She knew she should get home and start her homework. But the thought of stopping for a soft drink with Link was too tempting to turn down.

"Okay," she said. "But I can only stay for a few minutes."

The Burger Barn was almost empty when they walked in. The after-school crowd had already left.

Link led her to a booth in the rear of the shop. "What will you have?" he asked as she sat down.

"A lemonade, I guess."

He glanced at the big clock on the wall. "It's almost five-thirty," he said. "How about letting me buy your dinner?"

"I don't know," she said.

"Go ahead. Call your mom," he urged. "Tell her you're going to eat here with me."

"What about your mother?" she asked.

He smiled at her. "Don't worry, I'll let her know."

Dee didn't know how her mother would take the phone call. She had never done anything like this before.

She slid the dime into the slot and dialed. Dee wasn't sure what she would tell her mother.

"Hello?" her mother's voice answered.

"Hi, Mom," Dee began. "Listen. I'm here at the Burger Barn with Link. He wants me to stay and eat with him." She paused. "Is it okay if I don't come home for dinner?"

"It's not the healthiest dinner you could eat," her mother said. Then she laughed. "It's all right.

We were only having stew. Go ahead and have a good time."

Dee gave a sigh of relief. "Thanks, Mom. I'll see you in a little while."

As she hung up, Link took the receiver and called his home.

When they were settled back in the booth, he looked at her with a grin. "That wasn't so bad, was it?"

Dee shrugged. "I've never done this before — not go home for dinner, I mean. I wasn't sure how my mother would feel about it."

"And how did she feel about it?" He raised an eyebrow.

Dee laughed. "She didn't seem to mind at all."

He sat back in the booth. "That's because your mother likes me. All the mothers like me."

"Ha, ha," Dee laughed. "That's because they don't know you very well."

A waitress came to their table. It was a girl from their high school.

"Hi," she said. "What can I get you?"

"What have you got?" Link asked.

She handed them each a menu. "I'll be back in a minute."

Dee studied the menu. Most of the food was not on the diet that she followed carefully.

"What'll it be?" Link asked.

"I guess I'll have the fruit salad with cottage cheese," she said, "and a glass of milk."

He wrinkled his nose. "That isn't much of a dinner."

She closed her menu and put it aside. "That's what I want."

When the waitress came back to take their order, Link asked for a double cheeseburger with onions, and fried potatoes. He ordered a soft drink to go along with it.

"Ugh," said Dee. "Don't you care anything about your body?"

He flexed his muscles in his arm. "What are you talking about? I've got a great body. Just ask any of the girls in school."

"Well, you won't have it long if you keep putting that kind of food into your stomach," she said. "You're supposed to be a good athlete. You should know better."

"Come on," Link said. "Having a cheeseburger and soft drink once in awhile isn't going to hurt anybody."

"Doesn't the football coach keep you on a special diet?" she asked.

"Only during training," Link said. "And then he isn't very strict about it. Besides, I'm not really built to be a football player. Tennis and track are much more my speed."

"Then why are you on the football team?" she wanted to know.

"I like to play." He smiled at her. "Why do you play tennis?"

"Why do I play tennis? Why — why — " she stammered, " — tennis is almost my life."

For a moment his expression changed. "Yeah. I'd noticed that."

She looked at him, wondering what he meant. But he had turned and was grinning at the waitress as she brought their drinks to the table.

"Save me a piece of that chocolate cake," he said, pointing to the dessert tray. "Don't sell it before I'm ready. How about you, Dee? Should she save one for you, too?"

"No, thank you." Dee shook her head. "I don't eat sweets."

"I should have figured that," Link said. But his eyes twinkled at his words.

After they had finished their main course, the waitress brought Link's chocolate cake. He finally convinced Dee to have a dish of ice cream.

"That wasn't so bad, was it? he asked when she had finished.

"It was very good," she agreed. "But I don't plan to eat sweets too often."

"I'll tell you a secret." He leaned across the table, laying his hand on top of hers. "I don't indulge very often, either. But I do like to enjoy myself once in awhile." He raised an eyebrow. "There's nothing wrong with that, you know."

They walked slowly home on the warm May evening. The air was wonderful. When they reached Dee's front door, Link leaned over and quickly kissed her on the lips.

"See you tomorrow," he said, holding her wrist for a moment before he left.

Dee watched as he walked away. Then she sighed and went into the house. Time to forget about Link and get some of her homework out of the way.

"Hi," she called out, walking back to the kitchen. Her parents were still eating dinner.

"Did you have a good time?" her mother asked.

"Sure," Dee said. "We just stopped for a bite."

"How did practice go?" her father wanted to know.

"Pretty well," she nodded. "I beat Angie again."

"That isn't very hard to do." Her father looked at her. "You do that all the time."

"And Coach Riley set up the doubles team today." She told them about the two teams.

"I'll play you a game tomorrow morning if you like," her father said.

"Great." Dee jumped up. "I'd better get going on some of this work. We're going to practice doubles in the afternoon."

She hurried up the stairs to her bedroom, taking a few moments to shower and change into jeans. As she settled down on her bed with her school books around her, she began to think about Link. He was a good tennis player; almost as good as she was. And if he didn't quite measure up to her, it was because he didn't devote his life to tennis the way she did.

She leaned forward, hugging her knees. Her thoughts were about the future. Would she and Link both be tennis pros, making the rounds of all the big tournaments, always winning, always together?

She shook her head and sat up. Dee knew that that was her future. Unless Link changed his way of thinking, it would never be his. She made up her mind to talk to him about it the next afternoon when they met for the doubles with Angie and Alan.

Dee spent the following morning playing a hard game of tennis with her father. After a light lunch and a short rest, she was once again anxious to get back on the courts.

Dee was the first to arrive at the school courts. Link showed up ten minutes later, and Angie and Alan came together a half-hour later.

"Let's start playing," Dee called as the others showed signs of wanting to stop and chat before the game.

"Okay, lady slave driver," Link said. "We're ready."

For a moment his words hurt, until she realized he was only teasing her.

They took their places on the court and volleyed back and forth, warming up. Dee knew that the others would be willing to waste away most of the afternoon like this.

"Come on. Let's go," she called. "We don't have that much time to put it all together." Reminding them that the doubles finals were only a week away, she was able to get them started playing a serious game.

They were into the second set and Link was serving when Dee realized that he served a lot of net balls. They were getting double faults far too often. She stepped back toward the line and watched his next serve closely. It wasn't until he was ready to serve the last point that Dee thought she could see what it was he was doing wrong.

When the game ended and they sat down for a moment to rest, she said something to him about it.

"Do you double fault that often?" she asked.

Link looked at her. "Yeah. That's my big no-no," he said.

"Well, I'm not sure — " she said, " — but I think I know what you're doing. Come on." She jumped up and they walked back onto the court. "Serve a few and let me watch you up close."

He looked at her for a moment, then went ahead and served several balls. Half of them landed in the net.

"When you hit the ball, point your racquet this way. See?" Dee showed him what she meant. "You're dropping your wrist." She moved her arm through the serve.

Dee held his arm back up in the air and said, "Now, go ahead and hit it."

He tossed the ball up, and as he followed through she grabbed his wrist, feeling the slight turn he made as his arm came down across his body.

"That's it!" she cried. "Couldn't you feel it?"

She pulled his arm up in the air again and forced it down through the return, keeping his wrist stiff.

"Can you feel the difference?" she asked.

He smiled at her. "Do it again," he said. "It feels good."

For a moment she didn't understand. He took the hand that was holding his wrist and ran it up and down his arm. "Nice," he said.

Annoyed, Dee pulled her fingers away. "Can't you be serious? I'm trying to help you."

His face seemed to close up. "I know you are. And I'm trying to thank you."

"Well, you're going about it in a very strange way." She turned on her heel and walked back to the sideline.

"Sometimes you're unreal," Angie said as Dee dropped down beside her on the wooden bench. "He was only trying to — "

"I know what he was trying to do," Dee said.

"But this is not the time or the place."

Angie looked her straight in the eye. "This is also not the Wimbledon matches," she said, and turned back to Alan.

Dee felt as if the wind had been knocked out of her. Now she was getting it from all sides. All she needed was for Alan . . . or Coach Riley . . . to start in on her.

She jumped up. "Are we going to play any more?" Her voice sounded cold, even in her own ears.

Link glanced at the watch on his wrist. "I can give it another half hour," he said. "Then I'll have to get going."

"Ah," Alan teased him. "Big date tonight?"

Link laughed but he didn't answer, and Dee felt her stomach drop to her toes. Was Link dating another girl? She hadn't heard any rumors at school. But then, she didn't mix much socially with the other kids. Maybe . . .

A half an hour later Link tossed his racquet aside and wiped his face with a towel. "That's it," he declared. "I have to get going." He turned to Dee. "Can I give you a lift home?"

"Thank you," she said. "I came on my bike."

He nodded. "Okay. Well, see you people." He waved and went off, Angie and Alan following close behind him.

Downcast, Dee picked up her things and rode slowly home on her bicycle. Somehow the afternoon had not gone the way she'd hoped.

Sunday seemed to be a long day. Dee slept late and after a game of tennis with her father she settled down to finish her homework. Television seemed totally boring that night. By ten o'clock she was in bed, glad to have the day at an end.

The next morning she awoke with a great sense of somthing ahead. It was Monday, the first day of the tennis tournament.

When she got to school, she found a note taped to her locker from Coach Riley telling her to report at once to the gym. All of the members of the tennis team were there, and the coach made a short pep speech to them.

"You're all good," he said. "There isn't any reason why each one of you can't beat the opponents you'll be meeting today. By Wednesday I expect to have a few top winners out of this group. After all," he said, "you are being coached by the best there is."

They all laughed, knowing he was being funny.

"Seriously," he went on, "there's a lot of talent in this room and I am expecting a great deal from you. Everybody report on the front steps at one o'clock. The bus will take us over to the county courts."

As the meeting broke up, Link came over and slipped his arm through Dee's. "Busy weekend?" he asked.

She shook her head. "Tennis and homework," she answered. "That was about it."

He backed off and looked at her, his face empty of expression. "Is that how you spend your whole life?"

"Mostly," she said. "Why?"

"I don't know. I should think a pretty girl like you would be out on a date on Saturday night."

"Is that where you were?" she spoke out before she could stop herself.

He threw back his head and laughed. "I'm not a pretty girl," he answered. "And no, that's not where I was. Do you really want to know what I was doing?" he asked.

She really did want to know. She wanted to know who her unseen rival was. Although, how could she even think of another girl as a rival? Link did tease her a lot. He had never shown that he thought of her as anything but another date.

"Saturday was my dad's birthday," Link said. "We had a big party at our house. You know," he shrugged, "family and friends, that kind of stuff."

"Oh." Dee smiled at him, suddenly feeling as if a great weight had slipped from her shoulders. "I didn't know."

"Of course you didn't know, silly. How could you? You don't even know my father."

"That's right," Dee agreed. Then she laughed. "This is a crazy conversation," she said.

They had reached the door of the biology lab. "Well, I'm in here first period," Link said. "See you on the bus."

"Sure." Dee turned and walked away, aware that he was watching her as she walked toward her first-period room.

Dee won her match that afternoon. By Wednesday, she had eliminated all of her competition, winning the senior girls' singles trophy.

She finished in time to watch Link defeat his last opponent and walk off the court as the boys' winner.

Angie and Alan had both made it down to the last day but were eliminated in their final match.

According to school rules, the whole team had to return to the high school together by bus. Dee's parents had seen her win and then went on home in their car. On the bus, Dee fell into one of the seats and leaned her head back. She was exhausted.

She felt someone drop onto the seat next to her and opened her eyes to see Link smiling at her.

"Tired?" he asked

"Aren't you?" she said.

"Yeah." He lifted his feet in the air and shook them. "Knocked out." He ran his fingers lightly over the trophy on his lap. "Nice, isn't it?" he asked quietly.

She smiled at him. "I'm proud of you. You played well today."

"Thanks to you." He looked at her. "You're the one who caught what I was doing wrong. Hey, you do look beat!" He slipped his arm around her so that her head rested on his shoulder. "That's a lot more comfortable than that crummy seat back," he said.

Catcalls echoed around them from the other members of the team. "Look at the little lovebirds," one boy teased. But Link didn't listen to them. He only smiled at Dee.

"Don't listen to those peasants," he said. "They're just jealous."

"Of me or of you?" she asked.

He lifted his trophy slightly. "Of this," he said.

When she looked at him she realized he was serious.

"Don't you think they all wanted this?"

Dee's fingers touched her own trophy, nestled beside her on the far side of the bus seat. Of course it was what they all wanted. That's why you played tournament tennis — hoping, believing that you would be a winner.

"And now we'll win the doubles for the school," she said.

Link shrugged. "I hope so."

She sat up and looked at him. "Are you telling me that it's more important for us to win our trophies than to win for the school?"

"I didn't say that." Link settled her back against his arm. "Look, Dee, winning is great, but it isn't the only thing in this world."

"You seem to be enjoying your little trophy," she said dryly.

"Sure I enjoy it. And I'm happy that I'm good enough to be the winner. And maybe someday it will be that important to me. But right now there are a lot of other things in life."

Dee was quiet. There weren't that many other things in her life. She had never had time for anything but tennis and school. Now there was Link. She wondered how she could make room in her life for him.

Only four schools had teams taking part in the doubles matches. Angie and Alan were eliminated in the first round. Link and Dee won theirs without a problem. The match-ups for the next day were posted before the players left the county courts. Dee and Link were playing the team that had defeated Angie and Alan.

"They're super!" Angie said on the bus going home. "The best I've ever played against."

"Better than we are?" Dee was surprised.

"Well," Angie shrugged, "I'm not sure. But they really are terrific! You're going to have quite a match on your hands."

"Don't worry about it." Link settled back in his seat, laying his arms across the back of the seat. "Dee and I'll take care of them."

"You're the greatest, right?" Alan laughed.

"Sure."

Dee watched him out of the corner of her eye. He seemed very sure of himself. But she had noticed in their elimination round that he was slipping back into his old habit of twisting his wrist. The number of double faults had piled up, and it was only because they were much better players than their opponents that they had won the match.

"You want to watch your wrist tomorrow, Link," she said. "I noticed today that you're doing the same thing — "

"Forget it, Dee," he cut in abruptly. "I know what I'm doing."

She quickly sat back and didn't say anymore.

Link was right. She had no right to tell him what to do. She just hoped that he would remember the next day what she had tried to tell him.

Saturday, the day of the finals, was very warm and humid. Because it was the weekend, the play-offs began in the morning. They started with the junior high division. It was one o'clock before Dee and Link were on the court.

They had hardly begun to play when Dee realized that everything Angie and Alan had said was true. Their opponents were great tennis players.

The other team won the first set six to four.

Link and Dee managed to pull out the second set. But halfway through the third, Dee knew they were in real trouble. The boy and girl on the opposite court didn't seem to be tiring at all. Their serves and returns were almost as strong as they had been in the first game.

"Whew! I've just about had it," Link said when they stopped after the second game of the set to wipe their faces. He and Dee were already down two games.

"Link, please," Dee pleaded, "don't give up. We can still come back and win."

"I'm not giving up, Dee. But listen, those two are terrific tennis players. It's no disgrace if we lose to them."

"Yes it is." Dee stamped her foot. "It's a disgrace to lose to anybody."

"Hey, hold it!" He took her by the shoulder. "This is a game, Dee. It's not life or death."

"It's life or death to me!" she said. "I hate to lose."

"There's such a thing as losing gracefully," he said quietly.

"There's also such a thing as giving up in the middle." She turned away and went back onto the court.

They managed to win the next two games, but in the end the other team pulled out the victory. It was the first time in many years that Dee had lost a tournament game.

Dee dropped down on the side of the court, staring at the ground, her thoughts all confused. Link sat beside her. He ran his hand gently down her arm, but she pushed it away.

"It isn't the end of the world, Dee," he said. "I feel bad, too, but — "

She looked up at him. "You don't feel anything. If you had listened to me about your wrist, none of this would have happened."

His face grew cold and he stood up. "I'll see you on the bus." He walked away.

Dee felt an arm on her shoulders and she jumped to find her father kneeling beside her.

"Come on, kitten," he said. "It's time to go home."

"Daddy," she asked, "am I wrong to feel this way?" She straightened her legs and stood up, her hands grabbing his. "Link says it's just a game."

Her father looked at her. "To most people it is just a game," he said. "But to some people it's everything. You have to decide what part it's going to play in your life."

Dee shook her head. "I'm not sure I understand."

Her father held her hands tightly. "Dee, you're good. You're very good. You can be a pro if you want to. But only you can decide if it is what you really want. This is one time in your life when you can't have everything."

She backed away and looked down. "You mean I can't have Link and tennis."

"Not right now," her father said quietly. "If you really want to be a pro, then for the next few years you're going to have to put aside things like Link and dating."

She looked up at him. "What do you think I should do, Dad?"

"Whatever is right for you." He touched her cheek with his hand. "Whatever you decide is fine with Mother and me." He dropped his arm. "We'll see you back home." He smiled at her and walked away.

Dee crossed the empty court, swinging her racquet against her leg. All of the spectators were gone by now, and across the field she saw the rest of the team getting into the school bus.

She turned and took one last look at the court. "I can't give it up," she whispered. "I'm good. I know I'm good." She straightened her shoulders. "I have to give it a try. Even if I never make it, I have to give it everything I've got."

She turned and ran quickly toward the bus. Dee knew that Link would be waiting and exactly what she would say to him.

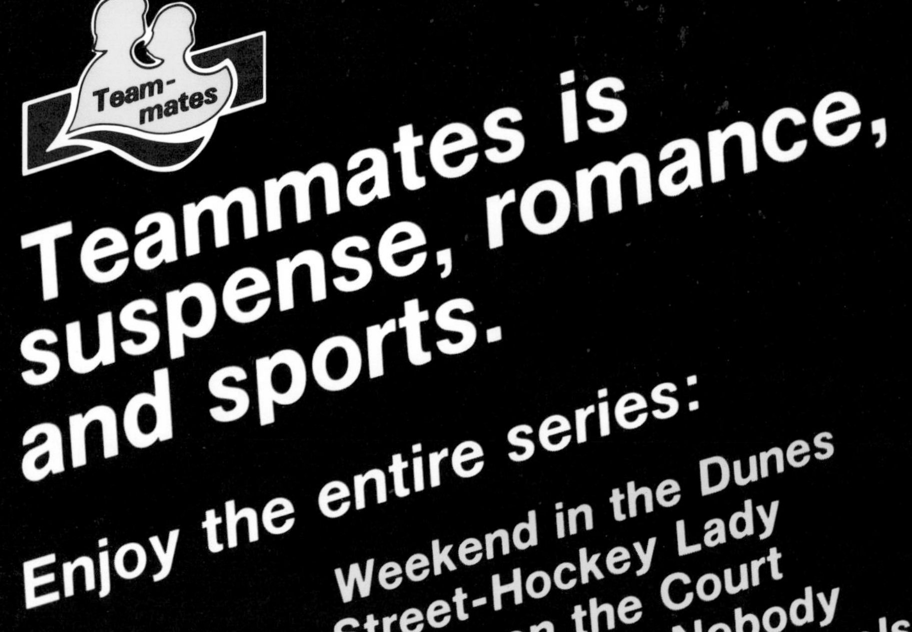
Team-
mates
Teammates is
suspense, romance,
and sports.
Enjoy the entire series:
Weekend in the Dunes
Street-Hockey Lady
Winner on the Court
Second-String Nobody
Partners on Wheels
Moto-Cross Monkey
Sarah Sells Soccer
Swim for Pride
Two at the Net
The Last Meet

Two at the Net
Second-String Nobody
Street-Hockey Lady
Swim for Pride
Winner on the Court